Harry the Poisonous Centipede's BIG Adventure

Harry the Poisonous Centipede's BIG Adventure

Another story to make you squirm

LYNNE REID BANKS

Illustrated by Tony Ross

HarperCollins*Publishers*

Harry the Poisonous Centipede's Big Adventure:
Another Story to Make You Squirm
Copyright © 2001 by Lynne Reid Banks
Illustrations copyright © 2001 by Tony Ross
www.harperchildrens.com

Library of Congress Cataloging-in-Publication Data
Banks, Lynne Reid, 1929–
Harry the poisonous centipede's big adventure / Lynne Reid Banks.
    p.   cm.
Sequel to: Harry the poisonous centipede.
Summary: Harry, a young centipede, faces danger and frustration when he
is captured by a hoo-min and placed in a jar.
    ISBN 0-06-029139-7 — ISBN 0-06-029394-2 (lib. bdg.)
    1. Centipedes—Juvenile fiction.   [1. Centipedes—Fiction.   2. Insects—
Fiction.]   I. Title
PZ10.3.B2155 Hat   2001   00-38832
[Fic]—dc21   CIP
                                                                      AC

1 2 3 4 5 6 7 8 9 10
❖
First Edition

To Dnl Stphnsn
(and his prnts)

To Dnl Stphnsn
(and his prnts)

Contents

1. Caught!

Harry was bored.

This is not something that happens often to a poisonous centipede. Harry was generally very busy about something or other. Chasing things like beetles, ants, and worms, biting them with his poison pincers, and eating them; running away from bigger things like snakes and rats trying to eat *him*; exploring in the tunnels; playing with George, his best friend; or just being at home in his nest-tunnel with his mother, Belinda.

As perhaps you know, Harry was not

1

his real, Centipedish name. This was (are you ready for this?) Hxzltl. And George's was Grnddjl. And Belinda's was Bkvlbbchk. They're hard to say. But then, so is any word, if you leave the vowel sounds out.

Try it with your own name. Bet you can't say it in Centipedish so anyone would recognize it. I mean, say your name is Daniel; in Centipedish (which leaves out the *a*'s, *e*'s, *i*'s, *o*'s and *u*'s) it would be Dnl. If your name's Rebecca, it would be Rbcc. If your name *begins* with a vowel, say Anna or Ursula or Oscar, it's even worse—I mean, how could you say Nn or Rsl or Scr?

But that's the way centipedes talk to each other—well, I say "talk," but it's more of a crackle. Too faint for human ears to hear. Often they just signal with their feelers. That's why they're rather strange, secretive, mysterious creatures.

You're really lucky to have me to tell you about them.

Where was I? Oh yes. Harry. Being bored for once.

He'd spent the early part of the night, since he woke up, helping his mother in their nest-tunnel.

He'd straightened out his leaf bed and rubbed his head on the earth floor to polish it.

Then Belinda had brought home a stag

beetle for their
breakfast, and he
had helped her get
its massive jaws and its hard carapace off
and had hauled them out to their rubbish-
tip tunnel. Then, while they ate, he asked
for a story and his mother told him one
about a family of marine centipedes.

"Once upon a time, beside the great
no-end puddle, there lived a family of
centipedes that could swim."

The stories always began like that.
Harry loved them. He thought marine
centipedes—his distant cousins—were
brll, not to say cl and wckd. But she cut
the story short at the most exciting part,
because she thought she heard something
interesting bumping about on the no-top-
world over their heads and scuttled off to
investigate it.

That left Harry, tummy full of stag
beetle, not feeling like moving much,

wanting to know the end of the story—
and missing George. Who was missing.

I mean, he'd disappeared. This was not
unusual. George was a free spirit. He
didn't have a mother (though he borrowed
Belinda when he was lonely or hungry).
No one to keep tabs on him and stop him
doing silly or dangerous things.

So quite often, he went off and had an
adventure on his own. Then he was
sometimes gone for nights. Harry and
George were getting to be big centis now
(a centi is a child centipede). A bit like
teenagers. So Belinda couldn't keep
control the way she used to.

Harry lay on the floor of the nest-
tunnel. He stretched himself to his full
length, which was now about five inches.
All his segments (he had twenty-one, with
a pair of legs on each, forty-two legs
altogether) felt lazy. And yet in Harry's
head was an urge to go somewhere, do

something, have an adventure. Only, what?

He let himself play with the idea of going along the forbidden tunnel and Up the Up-Pipe into the Place of Hoo-Mins. He and George had done that once, when the white-choke (which was smoke) had driven them out of their usual tunnels and they had had to climb into the Hoo-Min's home up his drainpipe and *very nearly* never came back again.

But no. That was too scary. Harry had a healthy fear of Hoo-Mins. Whenever he heard the vibrations of their great feet thudding overhead in the no-top-world, Harry cowered down or ran to hide (even though no Hoo-Min could see him down in the tunnels). George, when he was there, laughed at him and called him a sissyfeelers, but Harry couldn't help it.

His father had been killed by a Hoo-Min. So you can understand it. Even if

Hoo-Mins had not been the biggest, fastest, weirdest, scariest things around.

"Walking about on two legs like that," crackled Harry to himself. "It's not natural. They're not like anything else. They're not like hairy biters or belly crawlers or flying swoopers. They don't *belong*."

He had the vague idea that maybe they'd come from some other world. Not that he had any idea about planets and things like that. With his little weak eye-clusters he'd never even seen the stars. He just felt certain that Hoo-Mins were not part of the proper order of things.

They were just *too much*.

After a while, when Belinda didn't come back, Harry gave a centipedish sigh (which he did by making a ripple go all along his back where his breathing holes were) and got to his forty-two feet. He wandered up the nearest tunnel, and when he got to the end, poked his head idly out into the night air of the no-top-world.

If he hadn't been feeling rather dopey and full of food, he might have sensed something wrong and ducked back down again. But he didn't. The darkness was sweet smelling and the noises were all the ones he was used to—the faint sighing of palm fronds rubbing together, the rustle of little night creatures skittering about. Not even a night bird's cry alerted him to danger.

He crawled forward until half of him was outside the hole.

Suddenly the most awful thing happened.

Something tightened around his middle!

He almost jumped into the air with fright. He instinctively turned and tried to run back down the tunnel. But he couldn't. Something was holding him.

Something was dragging him!

SOMETHING WAS LIFTING HIM INTO THE AIR!

He threshed all his legs frantically. He twisted his head and closed his poison pincers again and again, trying to bite. But there was nothing *to* bite.

Only air.

The thing that had caught him was a loop of strong thread. It had been laid around the mouth of his exit tunnel. When he came out, the thread had been pulled sharply. The loop had tightened around him, between his tenth and his eleventh segments. Now he was dangling in midair on the end of the thread.

He was so frightened he didn't even try to see what had caught him. He felt himself twirling, first in one direction, then back again in the other. High above the ground. If centipedes could be sick, Harry would have thrown up.

Then he felt himself moving through the air. He was being carried on the end of the thread, but he didn't know that. All he knew was that never, since he had nearly drowned, had he felt so helpless and doomed.

I've been picked up by a flying swooper!

he thought despairingly. *I'm done for! Oh, Mama!*

But there was no Belinda to come to his rescue.

2. The Hard-Air Prison

Harry was carried, dangling and twisting, for some distance. Then there was a change.

Harry was used to the dark. He lived underground *and* he was a night creature, so he liked darkness.

And, except for that one time when he had been in a Hoo-Min's home, he had never been indoors. But that one time had made such an impression that when the sudden brightness came, and the smells all changed, and the natural night noises stopped, Harry knew immediately that he was once again in a Place of Hoo-Mins.

The most frightening place in the world.

He heard terrible, loud, un-understandable noises. They were Hoo-Mins' voices, but he didn't know that. He just knew he'd never heard anything like them. They were so loud they hurt his ear holes.

Of course, he couldn't know what they were saying. But you can know, because I'll tell you.

A little boy's voice said, "Look, Dad! I got another one!"

And a man's voice said, "Good for you, son! I told you you'd catch one with the thread if you were patient."

"Is there a spare jar?"

"Yes. Your mother washed out a big pickle jar. Put him in here."

And Harry felt himself going down. Down and down. But when his forty-two feet touched something, it wasn't lovely, friendly, soft earth. It was something hard and cold.

The loop was still around his middle. It was tight. It hurt him and scared him. But then there was a snapping sound, and he felt the pull of the loop go slack. It was still there, around him, but at least it wasn't pulling anymore.

The thread had been cut.

He tried to flee. He thought he could escape because he couldn't see anything in his way. But as he ran forward, he banged his head. He turned and ran the other way. After a very few steps, he banged his head again!

He turned sideways and ran. He found he was running in a circle. Every time he tried to turn out of it, he bumped into something—something he couldn't see.

He stopped, and touched the barrier with his feelers. It was weird. He could feel it but he couldn't see it. It was under him and all around him. It was like hard air.

He tried to climb it, but it was too slippery. His little claw-feet couldn't get a grip on it. He slid back.

"He can't get out of there," said the man. "But put the lid on just in case. I've punched a hole in it so he can breathe."

The little boy said happily, "I've got two centipedes in my collection now!"

A shadow fell on Harry, down in the bottom of the hard-air place. It was the lid going on, but he didn't know that.

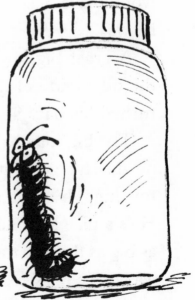

He crouched down till his tummy touched the cold stuff.

Harry had never heard a Hoo-Min talk before. But he began to guess that was what was happening. He could see them now, two of them, a big one—huge, enormous, vast, gigantic, the biggest live thing he'd ever seen—and a not-so-big one that was still huge, enormous, vast, and gigantic to Harry. He was terrified. If he could have understood their speech, he would have been even more terrified than he was.

A great big horrible face appeared on the other side of the hard-air wall. Harry turned his back so as not to see it.

The big man said, "Now you take care he doesn't get out. And don't dream of touching him. They're very dangerous. He's a nice big one, though, isn't he? Not as big as the one that bit me, though! That was twice his size."

The man didn't realize he was talking about Harry's mother!

"I hate the things!" the man went on with a shudder. "Take him to your room, quick, before I tip him on the floor and squash him to a pulp!"

"I think he's great," said the boy. "Almost as good as my yellow scorpion."

"You know what your mother thinks about all those creepy-crawlies in the house. Just don't let him out of the jar."

"Of course I won't," said the boy scornfully.

Then Harry saw a big pinky-brown THING wrap itself around the hard-air place. He looked down, and his weak little eyes could see the ground (it was a table, actually) sinking far away below him as the boy picked up the jar. It was awful, because Harry felt as if there were nothing underneath him to stop him falling.

He knew—he knew for certain—he was

going to get his wish for a major adventure. And he wished with all his little centipedish heart that he was safely back in his home tunnel.

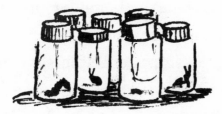

3. The Collection

Harry in his pickle jar was carried along for a short way, and then he felt a jolt and saw that there was something solid underneath the floor of the hard-air place. He lost his head and started trying to escape again, running around and around inside the jar. It was useless, of course.

Suddenly he stopped. He'd caught a signal!

Insects and other small creeping creatures can't speak to each other across the species, but they can make crude signals. I mean, one kind of creature can tell from another's behavior if there's danger, for instance.

Now Harry stopped helplessly running around, and looked through the clear wall. Not far away from him was *another* hard-air prison. And in it was something he recognized.

He recognized it because it was very like what he'd eaten for breakfast.

It was a beetle, a large one. Not a stag beetle. A dung beetle, a female. Dung beetles are only happy when they have a ball of dung to roll along. This dung beetle didn't. She had some earth in the bottom of her prison, but it wasn't dung, and she hadn't the heart to roll it into a ball. Anyway, there was nowhere to roll it to.

She just sat forlornly with her six legs bent and her large head lowered. She looked to Harry like two things at once: a sad lady beetle and a good meal. He didn't know which came first, but as he was still quite full of one of her distant relations, he decided to treat her as a fellow prisoner.

It was she who'd signaled to him. The signal said something like, "This is bad and I am sad." (Beetles talk and signal in Beetle, a language that always rhymes. Of course, Harry didn't grasp this, just the general meaning—I've translated from Beetle as best I can.)

Harry signaled back, "Same here."

She swayed her head from side to side. Then she moved forward and raised herself clumsily and put her front feet on the hard-air. This said, as clearly as words, "There is no doubt, I can't get out."

Harry rose up against the wall nearest

to her, putting his front eight pairs of feet against it. "Me neither."

The lady dung beetle swung her head in a wider arc. "*None* of us can. Have you a plan?"

Harry looked around. And got another shock.

There were lots of prisons made of the hard-air stuff! Harry couldn't count, but if he could, he would have counted ten or twelve glass jars on the trestle-table where his was. Each one contained a prisoner.

There was a yellow scorpion, nearly as large as Harry, with pincers a lot larger (though his poison was in his tail, just now lying dejectedly behind him). There was a rhinoceros beetle, his big curved horn resting against the prison wall.

There were several caterpillars of different sizes and colors. There were two or three millipedes, a large, hairy tarantula, and several smaller spiders. There was a stick insect, which looked very unhappy indeed—it could hardly stand up straight, and besides, it didn't have any sticks to hide among. Harry looked at all of them and took in their signals. All of the signals were sad and frightened.

And then he stiffened. Down at the far end, there was another centipede!

If centipedes could gasp, Harry would have gasped when he saw him.

It was George!

"Grndd! *Grndd!*" Harry crackled. But his crackle didn't go through the hard-air.

Harry began to run around his prison, frantically sending signals. The movement attracted the attention of all the prisoners. The ones who were lying on the floor of their jars—some sleeping, some just slumped in despair—stood up and turned his way. His turns, his twists, his liftings

and scrabblings of his front feet on the wall made all the others think something was up.

A sort of current, or wordless message, passed from jar to jar. The dung beetle passed it to the scorpion, who passed it with a curving of his poison tail to the rhinoceros beetle, who bumped his horn against the glass with a loud click, alerting the caterpillars, who wrigglingly passed it to the tarantula. She hugged the air with her furry front legs urgently. This passed the message to the other spiders in their own language, and their scuttlings and

jumpings passed it to the stick insect.

He was so depressed he couldn't be bothered to pass it on, but by that time it didn't matter. George had already grasped the fact that someone was trying to signal to him. He peered through his own glass wall and, though it was far away, he could just about make out some centipedish movements, which he recognized at once as Harry's.

(Centipedes might all look alike to you, but believe me, they can tell each other apart as easily as you can tell your mother from your worst enemy at school.)

"Hx! Hx! They got you, too! Hx, we've got to get out!" signaled George, twisting and turning frenziedly.

Harry picked this up with some difficulty and stood still. He thought about it for a moment and then, slowly and deliberately, he sent this signal:

"Can you tunnel through this hard-air stuff?"

George signaled: "No, and nor can any of the others. There was a mole-cricket here before, and *he* couldn't." The centis knew all about mole-crickets. They were among the best tunnel diggers in the earth.

"What happened to him?"

George lowered his head and sent a brief signal.

"Stopped."

No creature likes to think about death. They all have words for it that soften its meaning, the way we say "passed away."

But Harry had to ask.

"Did the Not-So-Big Hoo-Min stop him?"

"No. He just stopped. He—he'd been here a long time. He wouldn't eat. He didn't want to go on moving."

Harry shuddered all along his cuticle. Could anything so awful happen to him and George?

4. Captivity

There followed a long, long time of misery. Sheer misery.

Being in prison is horrible for anyone—or anything. Every creature alive hates it. But some prisons are worse than others.

The Not-So-Big Hoo-Min probably thought he was treating the creatures in his collection quite well. But he wasn't much of an expert, really. He liked catching things and then keeping them to look at, but unfortunately he didn't read much. So instead of studying in books how to look after his captive creatures, he just did what he *thought* was right.

He wanted them to stay alive, so he put some earth into their jars (but not enough to tunnel in), and sometimes some leaves and twigs and things to make them feel more at home.

He did give them water (which was just as well for Harry and George, as centipedes need to keep damp). But his idea about food was that all insects and other creepy things ate each other. So what he did was, he caught flies or cockroaches (of which there were so many in his house he didn't bother adding them to his collection) or else dug into ants' or termites' nests. Nearly every day he brought a whole mess of ants or termites and their eggs into his room on a shovel, and with the help of a large spoon, dumped them, along with bits of their nests, into the glass jars. Usually right on top of the prisoner underneath.

This was *fairly* all right for Harry and George, though they got a bit tired of eating the same thing every day. But for the caterpillars, who ate leaves—and only the leaves they liked at that—it was starvation time, and all but one of them *stopped*. (The one that didn't *stop,* stopped in another way: it turned into a pupa. George and Harry agreed that that caterpillar was lucky. Fast asleep and out of it.)

The stopping of the caterpillars made all the other creatures—including those who would gladly have eaten the poor caterpillars under ordinary circumstances—really angry with the Not-So-Big Hoo-Min.

"It keeps us here in woe and fear, so feed us good is what it should!" signaled the lady dung beetle angrily. She wouldn't eat the ants or their eggs or the flies either—what she liked was *dung* and all the tasty bits of seed that it contained, and she was having a pretty thin time.

Harry, scoffing cockroaches and termites' eggs, felt uneasy about her. To tell the truth, though he felt a little odd about it since he'd been brought up to think of her as food, he was getting to like her. It wasn't very nice to think of waking up one night to find her on her back with her six legs in the air.

He and George signaled endlessly about how to escape.

They remembered the earth pile that had helped them get Up the Up-Pipe. They piled the earth and remains of ants' nests against the clear walls of their prisons, and tried to climb up it. But the lids were firmly in place and the holes in them were too small to creep through.

"We'll just have to stick it out," Harry signaled to George. "At least we've got enough to eat."

"We'll get out somehow!" said George staunchly.

These signals, which some of the others picked up, had a cheering effect. Even the stick insect sat up and grabbed a fly.

The spiders, meanwhile, were all right (as long as the Not-So-Big Hoo-Min caught enough flies for them), except that they couldn't fix their webs onto the slippery hard-air, so they were bone idle and bored to death. But the tarantula—which was very big—simply wasn't getting enough to eat.

From time to time she leapt on everything that was dropped into her jar, becoming a blur of whirling stripy fur, and in a matter of moments, every fly, ant, termite, egg, or

cockroach had been seized and sucked dry or stuffed into her gaping jaws. Then she folded her long hairy legs up under her and lay still until her snack was digested. Then she rose slowly onto the tips of her legs and looked around at them all through the hard-air and sent this sinister signal:

"I am still *ravenous*, and if I could get at you, I would gobble up every last one of you!"

The scorpion retorted, "I'd like to see you try!" He pinched his claws and brought his poison tail up slowly and menacingly over his back as if he'd love to stick it into the tarantula's body. Then they did a sort of threatening dance toward each other, while the others watched.

It was extraordinary how well they could understand each other's signals now. Harry began to feel it might be rather difficult for him, if he ever got out, to make a meal of certain creatures ever again—dung beetles, for instance. He was very glad that there were no crickets or locusts (his favorite food) in the collection, or he might have gotten to like *them*.

Being a prisoner certainly made him think differently about all kinds of things. For one thing—his mother.

He found himself thinking about her a lot. The comfortable, safe home she'd made for him. All the treats she'd brought him. And he thought about the not-so-good things, too, how she fussed about danger and her crossness when *he* fussed about his food (he *hated* termite eggs and wouldn't touch them at home. Now he had to eat them and had realized they weren't so bad after all).

He thought about all her warnings, which had seemed so tiresome at the time. How many times had she told him never to go out to the no-top-world without her? But George did, so Harry did, whenever Belinda's back was turned. And now look what had happened. She'd been right all along.

He only wished he had the chance to tell her that. To say he was sorry. Because she must be so worried about him! Harry hated thinking about that, because he knew it was his own fault he'd been caught.

Now it was Too Late.

But what Harry did most was, he watched all the other creatures in their clear prisons, where they had no way to hide themselves and no proper, natural life. And sometimes he despaired. Unless something happened, the Not-So-Big

Hoo-Min would keep them all in prison until they *stopped*, and he would never see his mama or his home again.

This was a terrible thought.

5. Crash!

And then quite suddenly everything changed.

Since Harry had been caught, only the Not-So-Big Hoo-Min had ever come into the room where the collection was. The Big Hoo-Min never did. But one day— and it was daytime, Harry and George were asleep, their heads dug into the earth to hide them from the light—another Hoo-Min did come in.

It was the Not-So-Big Hoo-Min's mother.

The reason she didn't come into this

room much was because she was scared to death of all the creepy and poisonous creatures in her son's collection. She hated them.

But she was a very house-proud woman. She couldn't go on forever not cleaning her son's room, which was just as messy and dirty as most boys' rooms are if they're not cleaned.

So in she came with her broom and bucket and mop and other cleaning stuff and stood looking around with a frown and muttering *tut-tut-tut*. She got to work right away, tidying and sweeping and mopping, keeping as far as possible from the long trestle-table where the jars were.

But over this trestle-table was a window, and the window was filthy. She looked at the dirt on it (and the spiders' webs—the free spiders, of course, not the prisoners) and decided she simply had to do something about it.

So, sucking her stomach in and reaching with very long arms over the tops of the jars, she started washing the window.

Now, what she didn't know was that the window frame was rotten. This happens a lot in hot, damp countries (did I mention that Harry lived in the tropics?). Termites and woodworms can eat away at wood under the paint, or it can rot from the wet. And you don't even notice it until one day it just falls to bits.

So while the woman was busily washing the window, taking care not to touch the jars, there was a sudden crash and a cloud of dust.

The woman jumped back. Part of the frame had fallen down onto the collection table, knocking two jars off. Of course, the jars broke on the hard tiles of the floor.

Now I know what you're expecting.

You think those jars just happened to be the ones that held Harry and George.

Well, that's just where you're wrong.

They were the ones that held the scorpion and the tarantula.

You can't imagine the effect this accident had on the Not-So-Big Hoo-Min's mother. She let out a piercing shriek and jumped backward. As she did

so, she slipped on the wet tiles that she'd just washed, and sat down heavily on the floor.

In doing *this*, she kicked the bucket over on its side. A tide of soapy water flooded across the floor, carrying the scorpion and the tarantula with it—right up against the legs of the Not-So-Big Hoo-Min's mother!

The tarantula did just what you would do if you were being swept along by water and felt something solid beneath your feet. She at once clambered out of the flood. She scuttled toward the high ground, which happened to be the woman's stomach.

The woman screamed again and swiped the tarantula as hard as she could, making her briefly into a flying tarantula.

Meanwhile, the scorpion, which didn't mind the water so much but was finding everything rather alarming, had scuttled out of sight underneath the woman's apron. There he found a nice little pocket into which he crept. (Scorpions love the dark, and this scorpion hadn't been able to hide properly since he was caught.)

The woman scrambled hastily to her feet, her mouth agape, her eyes on the large hairy tarantula now scurrying across the floor. Little did she know, poor thing, that she had a very big yellow scorpion in the pocket of her dress. (Yellow scorpions, I ought to mention, are by far the most dangerous kind. Their stings can be fatal.)

The woman, shaking with fright, picked up her mop and attacked the tarantula, which raced for the shelter of the bed and hid under it. Luckily for her (the tarantula, I mean), that space was full of all kinds of boxes and toys and bits and pieces—a hundred good hiding places—and the tarantula soon vanished from sight.

The woman prodded and banged about with her mop, shoving the things here and there, but, finding nothing, she leaned against the wall. She felt quite faint. She was sweating, or maybe she was crying. Anyway she reached into her pocket for a handkerchief.

Not a good move.

The next second she snatched her hand

out with another piercing shriek. The scorpion was clinging to it with his claws. His sting was stuck into her finger.

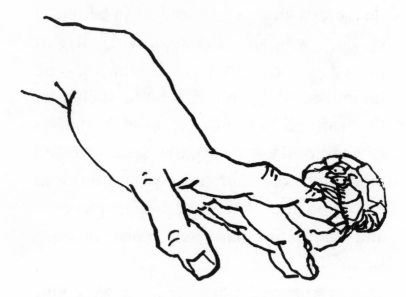

And that was when the big prison break happened.

6. The Big Prison Break

The noise and commotion had, of course, alerted the prisoners that something was going on. They had all woken up and were trying to make sense of what they could see. But they didn't have much time to consider it, because the next moment everything started to happen.

The woman was screaming and throwing herself all around the room. The scorpion let go and dropped to the ground, where her trampling feet (I'm sorry to have to tell you this) soon put an end to him.

In her pain, she forgot about the trestle-table with the collection on it and banged into it. It rocked, swayed, and tilted, and all the jars fell—or rather, slid—to the ground.

Most of them broke. Not all of them.
But Harry's did.
The prisoners fled in all directions.

Harry was in a terrible state. The fall, and the vibrations of the glass breaking, had scared him to death. Now he ran like mad away from the broken pieces of his hard-air prison.

He followed one of the millipedes and, for all its extra legs, soon overtook it. He knew about doors from his other adventure among Hoo-Mins, and, anyway, this door was open, so Harry dashed through it.

He was hunting desperately for a tunnel—a crack, a hole, anything. Then he remembered. The Up-Pipe! From this end, it was a Down-Pipe. If only he could reach it! He'd be home in no time!

He stopped running just for a moment to try to get his bearings. Behind him was terrible noise, vibrations, confusion. He looked around. He saw the lady dung beetle lumbering along some way behind him, spiders scurrying up walls, the millipedes' myriad legs rippling like mad. And then he realized: Where was George?

Every instinct told him to go on running—away, away from what had been his prison. Find the pipe. Zip down it. Home! Home was calling, pulling, *dragging* at him to keep going.

But he stood still.

The lady dung beetle, closely followed by the rhinoceros beetle, drew closer. *They* had not fled without looking—they couldn't, they moved so slowly. As they drew level with him, Harry sent a signal. "Other one like me—where?"

The rhinoceros beetle lumbered on, not even turning his head. But the lady dung beetle, whose signals he could read quite well now, said, "He's not free like you and me!"

Harry made up his mind. George had never left him in mortal danger.

He could not leave George.

He turned back.

A millipede ran right over him and sent him a muddled signal: "Are you crazy? The other way!" But he ignored this and kept going, back into the room, back into danger.

The woman, whom Harry now thought of as the Big-Noise Hoo-Min, was slumped on the floor now, clutching its feeler. Its noises were not as sharp as before, just a sort of whining sound like the wind down a tunnel. Harry sensed, with relief, that it could not attack him.

He passed the squashed remains of the poor scorpion. Harry paused to pay his respects. Without the scorpion, none of them would be free. He had *stopped* like a hero. Like Harry's own dad, who had *stopped* because he attacked a Hoo-Min to save Harry's mother, while Harry was still in his egg.

Harry found himself in the midst of big sharp pieces of hard-air and little piles of earth. He ran over and among them, hunting for George's prison.

And there it was! *There it was!* It was lying on its side. He could see George twisting and turning and butting with his head against the lid and the unbroken hard-air. His every signal said "Help! Help! Get me out!" Harry came alongside him and put his front ten feet against the hard-air. George saw him and stopped twisting and turning.

"What shall I do?" asked Harry frantically.

"How do I know! Just don't leave me!"

answered George, who, if centipedes could cry, would have been crying.

Harry didn't know what to do. All the other prisoners had escaped. He and George were the only ones left. Harry wanted to run. He *needed* to. He felt home pulling almost as strongly as the thread that had trapped him. He felt Belinda calling him.

But he wouldn't leave George alone. He couldn't.

He curled up on a tile, under the curved side of the jar. George curled up practically on top of him. They put their pincers together on either side of the glass and tried to signal comfort to each other.

It was all they could do.

7. Flying Through Space

They lay there together for a long time.

Things happened. The Big Hoo-Min came in and lifted the Big-Noise Hoo-Min up in his front legs and carried her away. The room was empty and quiet. Then after a long time the Not-So-Big Hoo-Min came in.

Even the centis could see from the way he walked that he was not happy. He crouched down by the fallen trestle-table and picked up some pieces of hard-air. Suddenly he saw the one unbroken prison, the one with George in it—the one with Harry under its curve. He picked up the jar. Then he saw Harry, and fell over backward.

Harry uncurled himself and faced the Not-So-Big Hoo-Min. He knew that if that Hoo-Min put its feeler out to touch him, he would bite it rather than be taken prisoner again. But then he would be stamped on like the scorpion. He would be *stopped*. How would he rescue George then?

He didn't have long to think about it. Before he knew what was happening, something dark came slamming down over the top of him.

He was trapped!

I don't know if you've ever tried to catch a bee that was buzzing against your window by putting a glass over the top of it, then sliding a card between the glass and the window. This was what the boy did, only instead of a glass jar (they were all broken) he used a box.

Soon, something thin slid under Harry's feet, and then the box with him in it was being lifted. The next thing was, he was sliding—falling! But not far. What he fell on was George.

The boy had slid him off the card into George's jar.

The lid was smacked back on. The two centis in the bottom of the hard-air prison looked out and saw the Not-So-Big Hoo-Min making a very loud noise out of a tunnel in its head. It sounded to them something like:

"YHRT MMTHR! HT Y! MGNG TPNSHY!"—which, if you work it out, is Centipedish for: "You hurt my mother! I hate you! I'm going to punish you!" (Of course he didn't talk Centipedish—that was just the way the centis heard it.)

Now, you'll say at once, "But it wasn't the centis who stung his mother at all—it was the yellow scorpion!" The thing is, when something bad happens to someone you love, you don't always get back at the right person (or creature). You just want to get back at *someone.*

The Not-So-Big Hoo-Min carried the jar, now holding both George and Harry, out of doors. It shouted at them a bit more. They noticed that the front of its big, round head was all wet and shiny.

(He was crying because his mother had been taken off to the local hospital and was very ill from the scorpion poison. In case you're worried about her, don't be. The doctors had the antidote and she didn't die. But, of course, her son, the Not-So-Big Hoo-Min, couldn't know that then. All *he* knew was that his father was furious with him for keeping the collection in the house at all. Well, I told you the wrong person sometimes gets blamed.)

All right. So the Not-So-Big Hoo-Min stood in front of its house and held the jar in its feeler and threw it with all its strength, as far and as high as it could.

Imagine the terror of the two centis as their hard-air prison went hurtling through the air! They'd sort of flown once before, when the Big Hoo-Min spat them out of its mouth (if you remember, from the first story), but this time they flew higher and farther than before. In fact they seemed to go on flying forever, with the jar turning over and over and making them tumble and bump around inside.

But at last there was a horrible jolt and shock, and the flying stopped.

They lay perfectly still for a long time, each wondering if he'd been bumped to pieces. But the jar wasn't still. It swayed and slid about a bit. Cautiously they uncurled and began running about. They could see the prison was on its side. And they didn't like the movements of it.

"We're not on the ground, Grndd," said Harry fearfully.

"Where are we?"

"I—I think we're high up in a tree," said Harry.

They were. It was a palm tree, and— perhaps luckily—they'd landed right in the middle of its clump of long shiny leaves. When it swayed, they swayed, and slid about in the slippery jar.

How were they going to escape?

It would have to be soon. Big-yellow-ball was shining down on them in a very fierce, hot way. They hated that. It blinded their weak little used-to-the-dark eyes. *AND* . . .

"Hx! I'm *Drying Out!*"

Drying Out is one of the worst things that can happen to a centipede. That's why they live underground where it's always damp.

Suddenly their prison jolted again, and a welcome shadow fell on them. I say "welcome" because it hid them from big-yellow-ball. But Belinda had always told Harry, "If a shadow falls on you, *run!*" And he couldn't. He could only crouch down in dread.

Something heavy and hard banged against the hard-air. It made a big vibration, so much that both centis almost leaped in the air. The bang came again— and again! It hurt their ear holes! It was horrible!

The fourth bang made a different

sound. They didn't know why, but something told them that whatever was banging on their prison was trying to *get* them and that that different sound meant the hard-air might be about to break.

Harry managed to look upward. Then he wished he hadn't.

Above him through the hard-air—which had a strange line across it now, a wiggly, jagged line—he could just make out what was causing the shadow.

"Grndd! Look!"

George looked up. "Wh- what *is* that?"

"It's—it's—it's the biggest flying swooper in the world!"

It was indeed the most enormous flying swooper he had ever dreamed of in his worst nightmares. It was glaring at him ferociously and hungrily, cock- ing its head from side to side.

What it
was, though
Harry didn't
know this, was
an eagle.

Soaring overhead, it had seen something unusual in the treetop, and it had swooped down to see what it was. There was nothing weak about the eagle's eyes. It spotted the centis the moment that its huge feet landed on top of the palm tree. And it at once determined to eat them.

So it banged the glass with its great hooked beak. Banged it and banged it. The fourth time it banged, its beak cracked the glass. But pickle jars are tough. It didn't break.

Now this kind of eagle does something rather clever with hard things that contain food. Like bones, for instance. It carries them high into the sky in its talons, and then, when it spots a handy rock underneath, it drops them and breaks them so it can swoop down and scrape out the good stuff inside.

The eagle reckoned the jar was a new kind of bone, a splendid kind that let you see the good stuff even before you broke it. So, it picked up the clear-bone (that's an eagle's way of thinking about a jarful of centipedes) and with powerful beatings of its wings, leaped off the top of the palm tree into the air.

It was flying away with the centis, fully meaning to drop them from a great height onto the first handy rock it saw.

8. The No-End Puddle

Ah! There was a perfect rock. Nice and flat, so the clear-bone wouldn't roll away. And with water all around it so that the wriggly things he wanted to eat couldn't escape.

The eagle was just taking aim and preparing to let the clear-bone go when he sensed danger and twisted his head.

Another eagle was heading straight for him!

He turned his great wings at right angles in midair to stop himself. Then he turned and faced his rival. Instinctively he spread his talons out in front of him to defend himself.

The clear-bone—the hard-air prison—the jar—loosed from the eagle's grip, dropped down and down, through the sunlit air.

The rock, like an irregular-shaped table, lay below. Waiting. The two centis curled up together, every segment clenched, hating the falling feeling. Though they didn't know it, the rock came nearer every split second! How could they avoid being killed by the terrible impact?

But it didn't happen.

When the eagle had been attacked, it had spoiled his aim. The jar missed the rock and fell into the sea.

And as it hit the water, the crack made by the eagle's beak came apart. The two halves of the jar flew into the air. The lid landed upside down on the surface of the water, with the centis inside its rim. Luckily, pickle jars often have deep lids. It was like a round boat.

A boat with a hole in it. The hole the Hoo-Mins had made so the captives could breathe.

Harry recovered first. He just knew that the water mustn't fill the lid. He saw it begin to come through. Instinctively he stuffed his back segments into the hole.

His tail end was in the cold sea, but the water stayed out. Their lid-boat, with them clinging to it, bounced about on the surface of the water.

George uncurled. He looked around. There was nothing to see but sea, and as he'd never seen the sea he didn't know what it was. Heaving green water under blue no-top air.

"Hx! Where are we?"

In a hollow, fearful crackle, Harry answered: "It's the no-end puddle, Grndd."

"No-end puddle? You mean, like in your mama's stories about marine centipedes?"

"Yes. She told me about it. That's how I know."

"Maybe some marine centipedes will help us!"

"Not unless we can get to the edge of it."

"But how can the no-end puddle have an edge if it's no-end?"

"I don't know."

"I thought they were just stories,"

crackled George. "I didn't think the no-end puddle was *real*."

A wave lifted them upward. They were on a water hill. They tried to look all round before they went down again into a dip. Harry said excitedly, "Grndd, I can see something not water!" He pointed with his front feelers.
"Are we going toward it?"

"I don't know—I hope so!"

They were lucky—the sea was calm. In a short time their lid-boat was washed quite gently up onto a smooth sandy beach. Before the no-end puddle could collect it again, Harry had wrenched his back end out of the hole, and the two centis had crawled quickly out of the lid and run as fast as they could up the sandy slope, away from the endless water.

"That puddle tastes terrible," said

George. "Yeuchh!" He rubbed his mouthparts against the sand to take the salt taste away, but the sand tasted just as bad. It was wonderfully damp, though, and the two centis set to work at once to dig enough of a tunnel so they could hide and feel delicious damp darkness all around them for the first time since they were caught.

9. To Eat—Or Be Eaten

They were so tired, they fell asleep curled up together in their shallow tunnel. They weren't afraid anymore, and they weren't in prison, and they weren't flying or bobbing up and down or drying out. It felt like absolute centipede heaven to them, after all they'd been through.

But when they woke up, they were hungry, and they remembered they were far from home and all alone in a very strange place. It wasn't quite such heaven then.

They emerged cautiously from their

tunnel. And straight away they got a fright.

The no-end puddle had crept up on them.

They had run a long way from it before going to ground. But now it was lapping and hissing on the sand, almost right under their feelers, like some vast creature about to swallow them. In a short time, if they hadn't woken up, it would have flooded into their tunnel and drowned them.

"Run, Hx! It's trying to get us!"

They ran away from it again. Higher and higher up the beach.

The sand got drier. It began to be hard to run.

"Stop, Grndd! The water doesn't come here."

George gave a centipedish sneeze, blowing the fine dry sand out of his breathing holes.

"Dare we go back a little way? This dry stuff's bad—I can feel it drying me out!"

They crept back nervously to the hard, wet stuff. The no-end puddle hadn't followed them. They began to run about, exploring. All around them on every side (except where the sea was) stretched sand.

Sand was enough like earth for the centis to understand it. They thought of it as sharp-earth because its grains were sharp-edged and not soft like soil. But this was more sand than they'd ever dreamed  of. It seemed as if all the sand in the world was here.

After a while they came back to each other.

"There's nothing here but sharp-earth."

"Did you meet anything?"

"No. It's empty."

"I'm hungry."

"Me too."

"If marine centipedes live here, they must have things to eat."

"That's right! Let's hunt!"

Now there was purpose in their running. They kept their heads low and their feet and feelers alert for vibrations.

At first it seemed to them that the  whole vast, flat expanse of sand was indeed empty. There were a lot of flies about. But they didn't land very often, and it was impossible to catch them.

The centis noticed that there were little holes in the sand.

"Maybe there's something tasty down there?" George suggested. He put his head right over the opening, and then wished he hadn't. A jet of filthy stuff came shooting out, right in his eye!

"Ugh! What a disgusting thing to do!" he crackled, wiping his face with his front legs. He sent a signal of reproach down the tube and got another eyeful of dirt for his trouble.

"That's too much! Let's dig it out and teach it manners, whatever it is!"

Together they dug into the soft sand. Straight down—taking turns till their tunnel was three times as long as themselves. Finally Harry, busily digging, bumped his feelers into something soft. He rushed forward, grabbed it in his pincers and dragged it out backward. When he got the tail tip of it out, George had to help, because it clung onto its hole like mad.

They got it out in the end. It was a worm, of sorts—a lugworm—and a fine feast they made of it, starting one at each end.

"That'll teach it to squirt its dirt in my eye!" said George with satisfaction.

They found several other holes and ventured into one or two of them, but in one they found a thing harder than the hardest carapace. They hollowed out a little sand cave around it and both tried to bite it, but it was no use. They had to give up.

"It wasn't a carapace—it was something else, as hard as the hard-air," panted Harry as they backed out into the no-top-world. "Some things certainly know how to make themselves safe around here."

They were still a bit hungry. They found a few hopping things that didn't hop quite fast enough. They were like a packet of chips to the centis—they nabbed them and crunched them up.

"That's better," said George. "Now, what do you say we—?" And then they felt something.

Something big.

They stopped and sent out signals in all directions. The vibrations got stronger.

Suddenly, George stiffened. "Hx! What's—"

It was coming! They could see it now!

But what was it? It wasn't a hairy biter. It wasn't a flying swooper. It certainly wasn't a belly crawler. And it wasn't a Hoo-Min. It was a—well, it looked to them a bit like a monster scorpion. But, no, it wasn't, even though it had enormous great claws like one. Whatever it was, it was horribly sinister, with little evil eyes that poked out on stalks. It had a vast carapace, much, much bigger than the biggest beetle, that stretched not front to back but side to side. It was as wide as the centis were long—*wider*.

It had giant mouthparts. As big as their whole heads. *Gaping*. And it ran on long jointed legs like a spider. It ran *sideways*. And it was bearing down on them.

Imagine a giant crab galloping toward you as fast as a horse. You'd be paralyzed with terror.

And so were the centis. They couldn't move. Not a leg, not a segment.

Not a feeler. It was too late to move.

The thing was almost upon them.

10. Rescue

At the very last moment—as the crab's monstrous claws opened to grab them—it suddenly stopped, lowered its claws, and turned around on its spiderlike legs. Its horrid eyes bugged out more than ever.

Something was happening behind it.

Harry and George, numb with terror as they were, peered between the thing's legs and saw a number of small creatures parading over the sand, almost under the eyes-on-stalks.

If centipedes' eyes could pop out on stalks, too, theirs would have.

"Grndd—look! Centipedes!"

And so they were. Smaller versions of Harry and George!

The monster had become confused. While its back was turned, the centis recovered enough to scuttle as fast as they could out of its way.

They made a big half circle on the sand and ended up face-to-face with the small centipedes that had saved them by distracting the monster.

"Come with us!" they signaled.

Harry and George needed no second telling. They ran alongside their smaller rescuers up the beach. Where the hard sand turned into soft, dry sand, there were piles of seaweed and other debris. The party of small centipedes dived underneath the pile, and George and Harry followed. It was very smelly under there, but at least they were hidden.

"Where do your tunnels start?" asked Harry as they pushed their way through the tangle of seaweed. The little centipedes could run under it easily, but George and Harry were too big.

"Don't have tunnels," answered the leader. "Live here under wrack." The centis had no idea what "wrack" was, but they guessed it was this tangled, smelly stuff. After pushing through it for quite a way, they came to a more open place. It was roofed with seaweed—wrack.

Harry and George looked at their rescuers. They weren't like them. Well, they were—they were centipedes. But they were different. Smaller. A different color. Fewer legs. A different kind of centipede.

They were, as you must have guessed, marine centipedes.

The first thing to do was to say thank you, and this Harry and George did. But their crackles were not quite the same as the marine centipedes', so they had to crackle it twice before they were understood. Even then, the small centipedes made it plain they weren't used to thank-yous.

They wanted to boast, though. They explained that they'd been tracking the newcomers. They'd tracked the monster, too. (They called it a side-runner, whereas George and Harry already thought of it as eyes-on-stalks—you see how different their languages were—but the centis knew what they meant, all right: a monster by any other name is still a monster!)

"When we knew that the side-runner had seen you and was going to charge," said one marine centipede called Drnblb (or, with vowels added, Dorunbelb. Or Darinbulb? Drainoblab? Shall we call him Danny?), "we decided to make a diversion."

"It was very brave of you," said Harry. "You saved our lives."

A female marine centipede edged up to them. At first they thought she was a centia (that's a female child centipede) because she was so small, but it turned out she was fully grown and a mother several thousand times over. Her name was Vrptkk. (Veruptikuk? Varoptikak? Well, let's settle for Veronica.)

"Are you hungry?" she asked, using the signal all centipedes use—a sort of knot-twist in their middles.

They both did a knot-twist to show they were. She signaled with her feelers that they should follow her, and led them to a large mess of something in a puddle of seawater. It looked like lumps of jelly to the centis, not at all what they were used to.

"What is it?" asked George.

"What *is it*?" asked Veronica. "These are sea-cucumber eggs. Delicious." She snuzzled her mouth into the puddle and sucked some up with a noise that made Harry think of Belinda's many reminders about table manners. (Of course, she called them mouthpart manners.)

The two centis tried to eat the eggs, but they were terribly salty and made them feel a bit sick. They asked if perhaps there was something else to eat.

"Oh, well, if you're fussy about your food!" said Veronica in a snooty voice. "Perhaps you'd prefer these." And she showed them some lugworms.

They were dead. In fact, they were rotten. They really looked awful, and they smelled worse. "Haven't you  any moving food?" George asked.

Veronica stared at him.

"*Moving* food? What *do* you mean?"

"I mean—something you stopped recently. Or something we can stop."

"You mean—you want to *kill* something?"

The centis were shocked. Centipedes hardly ever talk about killing. *Biting*— yes. *Paralyzing*—yes. But *killing* is what can happen to centipedes, it isn't what they do.

"We don't kill anything except in self-defense," said Veronica. "If you want to go hunting, like a—well, like a side-runner or a screaming swooper, you just go ahead, but don't expect *us* to help you."

George and Harry looked at each other in bewilderment.

"But in any case," Veronica went on, "there's not a lot to hunt on the hard sand: not much lives there except side-runners and, down deep, shellfish."

"What's that?"

"*What's shellfish?* Where do you come from? They're fish in shells. Like the side-runner, but with no claws or legs. Only they're no good till they're dead because they're shut in their shells and you can't get at them."

The two centis were shocked by the word "dead." To them it was the D-word.

"So what else do you eat?" asked Harry.

"We eat anything that's dead," she said casually. "Even side-runners, once the screaming swoopers have cracked them open."

"Why do you need—er—screaming swoopers? Can't you bite through their carapaces?"

"Carapaces? I'm talking *shells*. No centipedes, however *big* they are"—she gave them a sniffy look, as if being big made them somehow less centipede—"could bite through a *shell*. Of course, you can crawl in through their mouths," she said thoughtfully, "but we don't really care to do that."

The two centis shuddered. Harry

suddenly remembered the caterpillars that would only eat leaves, the lady dung beetle who wouldn't eat at all.

Would *he* rather starve than eat blobby jellified salty sea-cucumber eggs or stinking putrid long-stopped lugworms?

11. The Hunt

Veronica led them back to the others.

Harry and George didn't feel terribly safe out on the no-top-world with only a pile of seaweed above them. And the little sea centipedes were so *many*. Harry and George had never actually seen so many centipedes all in one place. Their kind of centipedes were rather solitary creatures—they didn't live in groups. But it seemed this kind did.

The sea centipedes had funny manners, too. They saw nothing wrong or strange about running all over Harry and George, examining them with their feelers, back and front, in the rudest way, and making remarks.

"Aren't they *gross!* And what an ugly color they are!"

"Yeah, funny smelling, too."

"Look at their long clumsy legs! Do you think they can run as fast as we can?"

"No-o-o, course not! Too heavy. And look—why do they need such big front claws?"

"They're for biting our prey," said George rather stiffly.

"And for digging," added Harry.

"What do you dig for? Lugworms?"

"We dig tunnels. To live in."

"You make tunnels—big enough for you?"

"Of course. And we're not full grown. You should see my mother," said Harry proudly. "She's as big as me and then as big as me again."

"That's a not-so," said a very small, cheeky sea centi.

"I don't tell not-sos," said Harry loftily. "It's true. A full-grown centipede of our sort is as big as an eyes-on-stalks—er—a side-runner. Spread out."

The little sea centipedes were obviously puzzled.

"What kind of centipedes are you?"

"Poisonous ones."

"Poisonous? What's that?" asked a lot of voices.

"What's poisonous?" said George. "It's—it's—" But he couldn't think how to explain.

"It's how we stop things for food," said Harry. "We bite them and paralyze them with our poison pincers." He opened and closed his a few times to demonstrate.

There was a stunned silence among the marine centipedes. At last, Danny, the leader of the group who had rescued George and Harry, multi-stepped forward.

"Show us," he ordered.

"Fine. What shall we bite?"

"We'll have to go out. It's all right—the side-runner's gone."

They trooped out from under the wrack. As they went, their party was joined by many more centipedes that came running. Soon there were swarms of them, running around George and Harry like schools of little fish around two big sharks.

The two centis could hear them crackling faintly to each other.

"Did you hear? They say they kill things!"

"They're going to show us how!"

George put his head close to Harry's.

"We'll show 'em what's what!" he crackled quietly. "Moldy lugworms, indeed!"

Danny led them away from the no-end puddle. They had to cross the dry sand. The sea centipedes were so light on their tiny feet they didn't even disturb the fine grains of sand, but Harry and George were slipping and sinking up to what we would call their knees. Luckily they soon found themselves under some palm trees where the sandy soil was quite firm.

Danny stopped and so did all the others. When everyone was still, they could all feel the vibrations from some creature nearby.

"What is it?" Harry signaled to Danny.

"It's a roll-a-lump!—Look! There he is!"

Harry's heart sank as he saw what it was. A dung beetle!—pushing its ball of dung along at a great rate.

Oh, no! Harry thought. How could he sink his poison pincers into something that had become a friend? But then he realized. Of course, this wasn't the lady dung beetle that had shared his imprisonment and learned to read his signals.

This was a great big ugly male, fairly bullying his dung ball along in front of him. He was signaling furiously in Beetle: "Out of my way, small creatures all—or I'll squash the lot of you under my ball!" He really was asking for it.

George didn't hesitate. He not only wanted to show off—he was hungry. He went into a crouch, and then with a strong war crackle he charged forward. Harry followed, but he wasn't needed.

George sank his poison claws straight through the beetle's shining black carapace, and the next moment, it lay on its back, paralyzed. The dung ball rolled a little way and then stopped.

The smaller centipedes were stunned for a moment. Then they rushed forward with centipedish crackles and signals of excitement.

"He killed it! He killed that huge roll-a-lump with one bite!"

They swarmed all over the prostrate

dung beetle, and all over George, too, not to congratulate him but because he was in their way.

"Let's eat it!" the younger ones crackled greedily.

"Hey, hold on!" said George. "We don't eat out in the open—it's dangerous. Anyway," he mentioned, "I—er—stopped it, so I think I should eat it."

This positively scandalized the marine centipedes.

"What! You mean, it's not for all of us?" asked several of the females reproachfully.

George felt abashed. "Well, of course

you can have some, too," he said. "Only, as I killed it—"

"Grndd! You crackled the K-word!" muttered Harry.

12. the Battle

Hardly were the words out of George's mouth about sharing his prize than it disappeared under a wave of small, hungry centipedes. In a trice, everything except the thinnest of its legs had been eaten.

Harry and George stood by, amazed and indignant, especially George.

"What's the matter with these centipedes?" he exclaimed. "Talk about bad manners! Your mama would have a centi-fit if she could see what they're doing to *my* dung beetle!"

Harry waded in and grabbed two discarded legs, which he carried back to George. "We might as well have a snack, anyway," he said.

But George was outraged. "Not me! I'm not touching their rotten leftovers!"

"Well, let's go and hunt something for ourselves," said Harry sensibly. There wasn't much meat on the spindly legs, and he dropped them and set off at once, with George just behind him.

But suddenly Danny was in his path.

"Hold on!" he said in his bossy way. "Where do you two think you're going?"

"We're going hunting," said George shortly.

"Fine. We'll follow you."

"Oh, yeah? What for? You're not much help as you won't k-kill anything." He was too angry to hold back the swear word.

"The roll-a-lump really wasn't enough for all of us. We'll share the next thing you kill."

Harry and George were flabbergasted.

"Oh, I see!" said Harry. "So you lot are just going to run around after us, eating our prey! Is that the idea?"

"What's wrong with that? We always eat what others kill."

"Forget it," said Harry. "Thanks for saving us from the eyes-on-stalks, but from now on, I'm going to eat alone."

"That goes for me, too!" said George, and the two centis set off at a run.

Danny had to scuttle aside. But he was signaling like mad to his followers, who, leaving the shattered remains of the dung beetle, marshaled before him like soldiers. At Danny's signal, they surged forward.

It was amazing how quickly that brigade of centipedes could move!

George looked back and saw them coming—a lot of them. Like the no-end puddle racing to engulf them.

"Faster, Hx! They're after us!"

George and Harry put on speed and fairly shot along the ground. But it was no use. The tiny centipedes split into two parties, encircled the fleeing centis

with a pincer movement (the natural tactic for centipedes, of course, a *pincer* movement), and before our heroes could dodge or find a hiding place, they were surrounded.

"Keep going, Grndd, they can't stop us!" signaled Harry.

But that's just where he was wrong.

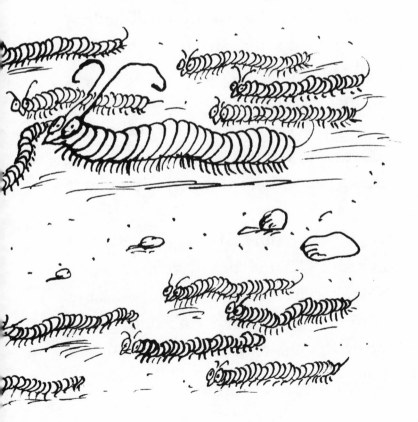

The little sea centipede army could stop them, and did.

How they did it was simple—they over-whelmed them with numbers. They piled up in front and behind, they swarmed over them, they nipped them with their tiny, non-poisonous pincers. In a very short time, George and Harry, bitten all over and weighted down by small bodies, had to give up the struggle—though I have to tell you that by the time they did, a number of their distant cousins had been *stopped* by poisonous bites given, reluctantly, in the heat of battle.

Danny stood before them, triumphant but furious.

"You *killed* some of us!" he crackled ominously. "That settles it. You're staying with us. You'll hunt for us and make sure none of us goes hungry. And don't think of trying to escape. We may be small, but we have powerful friends."

"Like who, for instance?" panted George defiantly from underneath ten or fifteen small centipedes.

"Never you mind. Let's just say, not all side-runners and screaming swoopers are our enemies."

"That's the biggest not-so I've ever heard!" crackled Harry.

"Are you prepared to take a chance on it?" asked Danny nastily. "All right, everyone. Back to the wrack with them!"

13. Sink or Swim!

Harry and George were chivvied and hustled back down the beach. George tried to make a break for it—just once. A mass of centipedes rushed on top of him and nipped his rear end until he came back into line.

They were heading back for their home wrack when suddenly Danny halted them.

"Look out! Screaming swoopers ahead!"

The sounds of seagulls filled the air. A number of the big birds were standing in

the wrack, stabbing it
with their beaks. What were they
eating? Sea-cucumber eggs or . . . ?

"Quick! That wrack over there!"
signaled Danny.

The whole crowd made a dash for
a dark patch of seaweed almost at the
edge of the no-end puddle. They had to
run a long way to reach it, and the
screaming swoopers had a field day,
screaming, swooping, and pecking. About
a quarter of the marine centipedes were
snapped up. But clearly the screaming
swoopers didn't feel like tackling George
and Harry, who, with every screaming
pass of the attackers, rose up threateningly
to defend themselves.

As soon as they were under the wrack, they spread out to make a smaller target for the gulls. But Danny (who had survived) ordered them to guard the prisoners.

The little sea centipedes started running around them like mad, forming a sort of living fence so that they couldn't run away.

"This is worse than the hard-air," said Harry. "At least it didn't bite you, and we had enough to eat. I'm *starving!* "

"Me, too. I might even be able to eat those disgusting sea-cucumber eggs!"

Veronica, who'd been put in charge of them, heard this. "So you've given up your fussy eating habits, have you?" she asked. "Come along then, I've just seen a lovely rotting swimmer you can have."

She herded them ahead of her till they came to a stinking dead fish.

"It's no use," crackled Harry very softly. "I can't face it."

"I can," said George, and proceeded to tear into the putrid flesh, eating as much as ten marine centipedes could have, and in half the time.

"You are a very greedy centi," scolded Veronica when she saw how much he'd eaten.

"That's a good one, coming from a sea centipede!" muttered George, wiping his mouthparts with his front legs. "Ugh, that is filthy muck! What I wouldn't give for a good locust! Hx, we have got to get out of here!"

"Don't worry, we will," said Harry, with a confidence he didn't really feel. "Next-night. I'm too tired to think about it now." He turned to Veronica. "Where are our leaves?"

"Your whats?"

"Our leaves, to sleep under."

"I don't know what you're talking about. We just sleep wherever we are."

"How uncentipede," muttered George. "Really, these creatures are so *worm*," he added privately to Harry, using the Centipedish expression for the lowest form of life. "I'm ashamed to be related to them."

Danny came hurrying through the tangle of wrack. "You'd better sleep here for today," he said. "You can leave them, Vrptkk. We'll guard them from the land side—they can't escape into the Big Lap. Then next-night we'll take them out hunting. They're going to be really useful!

We'll all have some new tastes." He didn't seem at all upset at having lost so many of his followers to the screaming swoopers.

Danny and Veronica hurried away, and a number of centi-guards took their place. They made a double semicircle around them on the land side. On the sea side, the waves were lapping the seaweed, moving and lifting it, then letting it sink back on the sand. It was as if the water breathed, like something alive wanting to eat them.

They briefly considered trying to run away, but they knew the guards only had to signal and help would arrive in endless numbers.

"We can't escape now, not with the no-end puddle against us," muttered George to Harry. But Harry surprised him.

"I don't see why not," he said. "We could just make a dash for it."

"A dash for it? Where?"

Harry stiffened himself. "Straight into the no-end puddle."

14. A Short Chapter with a Surprise at the End

Now you may remember that in the first story, Harry taught himself to swim, and managed to rescue George from a flood. Once you can swim, you never forget it.

Without giving himself time to get scared, Harry rushed forward, straight into the oncoming waves.

He was at once out of his depth. But he refused to panic. His little legs threshed, sending him forward. It's much easier to stay afloat in the sea than in fresh water.

He soon swam clear of the seaweed.

He didn't exactly *forget* about George. He just forgot George couldn't swim.

Poisonous centipedes are not natural swimmers. And George was terrified of water because of having once nearly drowned. When he saw Harry's back feelers disappearing into the lapping wave, he felt completely abandoned.

"Hx! Hx! Don't (*glug, blub*) leave me!" he spluttered as the salty water pushed him backward. But Harry had gone.

Did George dare follow him?

George backed up until he was belly deep in rotting fish bones. Behind him his escape was blocked. The centi-guards started nipping at his back segment. They had already sent runners to announce that Harry had escaped. Soon many more sea centipedes would arrive and move George to a place far away from where he'd last seen Harry.

They might never find each other again!

There was only one thing for George to do, and he did it. He didn't let himself think about it. With great bravery, he threw himself forward into the no-end puddle.

The next second he was in the sea! He was drowning!

But no! He felt his body shoot to the top of the water. He blew the horrible salty stuff out of his breathing holes. Just then, he heard Harry's crackle:

"Wriggle your legs, Grndd! Swim! Go for it—it's not far to the edge!"

George wriggled his legs like mad. His one aim was to keep his back out of the water. His head went under a couple of times but that didn't matter. He was moving forward! He was swimming!

And at last he felt himself seized and dragged. Harry, already on shore, had

seen him coming and had plunged back in to help him. In a very short time, both centis were sprawled on the sand just above the waterline, their breathing holes popping with tiny bubbles as they breathed. George was amazed at how far they'd swum. The wrack was a long way off.

"We made it, Grndd! We can swim as well as any marine centipede!"

And then they looked at each other.

"Why didn't they swim after us?" they asked each other.

Harry had always thought of marine centipedes as wonderful, fearless swimmers, but he was wrong. *This kind couldn't swim at all.* If Harry and George had but known, their cousins were, at that moment, running around in a complete panic. There's very little tide in tropical waters, but there is some, and the sea centipedes always hid under wrack that was high above the waterline. Now they were scurrying about frantically under the seaweed, which was beginning to float away. I'm afraid not all of them managed to escape. A number of them were carried away by the waves.

Of course, it was rather *worm* of them to treat Harry and George so badly. I'm not saying they deserved to drown (most of them, including Danny and Veronica, were all right), but don't you think it's rather interesting that it was the two nonmarine centipedes who were able to save themselves by swimming, while the *marine* centipedes couldn't?

15. The Long March Begins

The two centis dragged themselves up the beach. If an eyes-on-stalks, a screaming swooper, or anything else had attacked them at that moment, they couldn't have put up much of a fight, or even run away very fast. But luck was with them— nothing did.

After a long crawl, they found themselves once again among palm trees. The ground under them was firm and diggable, if they needed to dig. They wanted to. They wanted to make themselves a tunnel and crawl into it and never come out again, to face all the dangers and hardships they'd found out about. But there was something they wanted more.

"Grndd. Stop a bit."

George stopped.

"Where are we going?"

"Where do you think?"

"Home?"

"Of course."

If a centipede could be homesick—wait a minute, what am I talking about? *Of course* centipedes can be homesick. Most creatures can. They crouched down, every little segment filled with longing.

"I want my mama," crackled Harry very softly.

George said nothing. He wanted her, too.

"But how can we find our way back?"

George still said nothing. It was a

terrible question. He hadn't the slightest notion of the answer.

"Let's think."

They thought. George said, "How far do you think the giant flying swooper carried us?"

"I don't know. It seemed to last forever."

"No it didn't. I was looking down through the hard-air. We went over a bunch of trees. Then it was the no-end puddle, only I didn't know what it was then."

Harry looked up. "Mama knows about the no-end puddle. She might even have seen it, or how could she tell us stories about it? Maybe we're not so far from home."

"But how can we find it?"

Harry said slowly, "It's got a smell all of its own."

George realized this was true. When

they'd been out exploring the no-top-
world, they always knew how to find their
way back—as long as they didn't stray too
far from their home tunnel.

"Put your feelers up. See if you can
sense it."

They ran here and there, sensing and
smelling with all their might. But they
didn't get even a whiff of the dear,
familiar scent.

"It's no good. We're too far from it."

"So what can we do?"

"We'll just have to march away from the no-end puddle. Then maybe we can—" But Harry didn't know how to go on. He had no idea what they could do. He thought of them wandering about for the rest of their lives, looking for home, looking for Belinda. Facing dangers, being hungry, being frightened and lonely. Maybe never, ever finding what they were looking for.

It was such a terrible thought, he didn't want even to start. He felt all his hope and his energy draining out of him, like water out of his breathing holes that time he was washed ashore upside down.

But George wouldn't let him give up.

"Oh, come on, Hx! Remember your dad, what a brave centipede he was! He'd be so proud of you if he knew what you've come through already. I wouldn't give up if I had a dad like that, a-centipede-who-tackled-a-Hoo-Min!"

Slowly Harry pressed down on his forty-two feet and lifted his body.

"Right, Grndd. You're right. Let's get started."

16. The Worst Things in the World

They crawled and ran and rested and crawled more until dawn broke. And something else broke, too. No, it wasn't their backs—aching and weary as they were from their long march. It was the weather.

Where the centipedes lived, there weren't four seasons, as most of us have. There were just two—the rainy and the dry.

For all of Harry's and George's short lives, it had been dry. And hot. Very hot. But while they'd been marching through the night, there'd been a change. The sky had become heavy with clouds. They didn't know this, but they did feel the change in the air. And they heard rumbles of distant thunder. These had made the two centis crouch down in fear, but apart from a cool, damp breeze (which was pleasant), nothing had happened.

Now, quite suddenly, it did.

A big splosh of water fell on George. He stopped short, shook himself, looked around crossly, and then started forward again, though his legs would hardly hold him for tiredness.

Next, another big splosh—this time right on Harry's head.

If centipedes could sneeze, he would have sneezed.

"What's going on?" they both said at once. Because now there were sploshes all around them, sending up little fountains of dust as they hit the dry ground. They looked around anxiously. Had the no-end puddle somehow flown after them? Was it out to get them, drop by drop?

But the water wasn't salty. And suddenly Harry knew what it was.

"It's the Great Dropping Damp!" he crackled excitedly. "Mama told me about it! She says old-yellow-ball sends it when he gets fed up with shining! She said when it comes you have to go underground or it can wash you away!"

By that time they were nearly exhausted. Their legs would hardly hold them up, their cuticles felt like a coating of stone, their feelers drooped, and they were too hungry to feel hungry anymore. But the rain was now falling in torrents and they had to do something quickly.

Harry led the way up a slope. "Mama said if I was ever caught in the Great Dropping Damp I should get under something and find a tunnel!" he said importantly. George, blowing rain out of his breathing holes, followed silently.

They struggled through the heavy sploshing drops that were now falling all around them and on top of them. They were in luck. At the top of a slight rise was a jutting rock that made a shelter from the rain. Underneath it they found a ready-made tunnel—quite a short one, probably dug by a beetle or a mouse, ending in a little round nest-cave. It was quite dry there, though they could hear and smell the rain soaking the earth. With centipedish sighs of relief, they rubbed the wet off their cuticles and curled up together.

While they were asleep the rain stopped—for the moment. That's how the rains are, in the tropics. They start—they stop—and then, when they start again, that's it—it rains for months. But the centis didn't know that. The drumming sound stopped, and it was peaceful and still. And then—George suddenly woke up. He reared up and bumped his head.

"Hx! Wake up! What's that?"

Harry woke up and listened or, rather, felt. There were strange vibrations. It wasn't the rain falling. And it wasn't just one creature walking, slithering, hopping, or crawling on the no-top-world. It sounded like masses of tiny things. So many that the vibrations covered a huge area.

"Is it the marine centipedes? Are they after us?"

They were coming closer, whatever they were. Soon they would be right over where the centis huddled in their earthy lair.

"Quick, Hx! We'd better block the mouth of the tunnel!"

They started toward the entrance. But it was too late. The invaders were already there.

They marched in file, two at a time, down the tunnel. Harry and George stopped short, frozen with fear.

It was the most dreaded thing in the world.

Soldier ants!

Soldier ants are absolutely terrible. Even Hoo-Mins are afraid of them, and so is every other creature in the tropics. They can bite and sting, and every now and then they leave their nests, millions of them, and march through the forest, overpowering, killing, and eating every living thing in their path. Nothing can stop them except fire. And there was no fire here.

The ants were on the march.

Belinda had warned the centis about them many times. She told them: "If you sense them coming, run. Get out of their way. Or go deep underground, though they may follow you. If they corner you, there's nothing for it but to fight as long as you can."

Harry and George turned tail and fled, but there was nowhere to flee to. As they came up against the back wall of the nest, they had to stop because there was no time to dig any deeper. They turned again. They were trapped. The soldier ants were coming. The leaders were halfway down their short tunnel.

Harry was perfectly sure they were done for. But he said, "We must fight! Don't let them come into the cave. Let's block the tunnel!"

They had only a few seconds. They began frantically throwing earth to form a wall at the nest end of the tunnel. When they'd partly blocked it, only one ant at a time could crawl over it.

The centis prepared for their last fight.

As the first soldier ant poked its feelers and then its head over the barrier of earth, George lunged at it. He was shocked by the size of its head. It was far bigger than

an ordinary ant, and this was due to its huge, ugly jaws, which were open to bite. But George got in first, and snapped its head off with his poison pincers. Harry did the same with the next one.

The bodies helped block the tunnel. But others were behind them. They swiftly carried the bodies back along the tunnel, passing them from ant to ant, while other ants tried to get into the cave.

As fast as Harry and George dealt with them, so the bodies were cleared and more ants poured down. The centis knew that even though the ants were small, they could do what the marine centipedes had done—overwhelm them with numbers. They would just smother the centis' breathing holes and then bite them to death.

The vibrations overhead were now shaking the earth. These were not the soldier ants. They were driver ants—the main body of the ant army. The soldier ants were their guards. They marched in thick lines alongside the phalanx of marching drivers. The coming of the rains had triggered them to start marching through the forest, looking for food and a new nest site.

You might not feel the shaking caused by so many million tiny feet, but to the centis it sounded as a machine drill would to you. The vast army of ants were passing over the top of the centis' nest-cave in their countless millions. Every ant the centis killed, they knew could be replaced by scores of others.

It was hopeless. All was lost!

But they battled bravely on. They had no hope, but they were not going to give up easily.

As they fought frenziedly, killing ant after ant, something changed. The drumming vibrations over their heads got less and then petered out altogether.

As if at a signal, the invading soldier ants turned away.

Their marching column had gone past. Those attacking the centis had to go, too. Suddenly, there were no more ants. No bodies even. They had all gone, as if they had never been there.

The two exhausted centis stretched out side by side. They'd gotten a few stings but nothing much. The worst thing was the awfulness of having been so afraid. It took them a long time to get over that.

And of course they were dreadfully tired from the battle.

They managed to stagger up and block the tunnel entrance, and then they fell into a deep sleep until evening.

17. An Old Enemy

When night came, they woke up.

They were desperately hungry. "Those foul soldier ants might have left us just one or two of their stopped ones to eat," complained George. "We earned them!" They pushed their way through the earth block and tested the night air with their feelers. They could smell the hated smell of the driver ants' column from all the droppings they'd left. They saw how everything that had been in their path had been eaten.

"Nothing left for us, not even a head,"

said Harry gloomily. "Oh well. We'd better get on our way."

"Can you still sense the no-end puddle behind us?" asked George.

"No. It's too far away."

"How are we going to keep going in a straight line?"

"Is home even *in* a straight line? The giant flying swooper could have flown crooked."

"We'll never find it."

But now it was Harry who kept George's hopes up.

"Yes, we will. I know we will. There are other things that roam, besides the driver ants, things that don't have homes like we do. They travel around. Maybe they've seen Mama. She must be looking for us."

So they started forward again.

It's very hard, when you're small and close to the ground, to know which way you're going. Even Hoo-Mins can walk around in circles when they don't know their way, and *they've* got the sun to help them, and maps and landmarks, and they have binoculars to see far away. The centis just had to keep on plodding along through the underbrush, over and under everything that was in their way, hoping for the best.

But then they had a bit of luck. Not that it looked like luck when they first saw it—quite the opposite!

They heard it coming and dived under some dry leaves to hide. It was a single thing this time, not hoards of ants on the march. They heard it tiptoeing here and there, hardly causing any vibrations, but making a very faint rustling. It sounded as if it, too, might be lost.

Harry peeped out from under a dried palm frond. The tree it came from was nearby, and he was ready to run up it if danger threatened. And it did! Because he could see the thing now. It would scuttle a little way. Then stop and wave its feelers about. Then scurry a little nearer. It looked fearsome—large and hairy and stripy and horrible.

"It's a tarantula!" crackled Harry into George's earhole. "Up the tree—quick!"

They came out from under the dry stuff and rushed up the tree. Some palm trees, if you've noticed, have sticking-out bits on their trunks. They were like little balconies to the centis. As they climbed, Harry had an idea.

"If we climb right to the top," he said, "we might be able to see something."

"Like what—a hole in the ground?"

"Don't be so smart. No. Like the Hoo-Mins' nest where we were caught. If we could find *that*, we could get home easily."

Of course, the centis had no idea about houses, but they knew that the place they'd been shut up in stood up from the ground quite a long way. Harry had even caught a glimpse of it as the Not-So-Big Hoo-Min had prepared to throw them up into the tree.

So they climbed nearly to the top of the palm tree. They lay out along two of the sticking-out bits on the trunk.

The tree was taller than most of the others. The house they were looking for was actually in plain sight, not very far away. But of course the centis, with their weak little eye-clusters, couldn't make it out.

"I wish *we* were friends with a flying swooper," said George, peering about uselessly, "like Danny said he was."

"That was a not-so," said Harry. "No centipedes could be friends with a flying swooper. He was just trying to scare us."

Just then they heard something coming up the tree after them.

They instantly reared up their first eight segments to be on guard, and looked straight down.

Climbing slowly and carefully up the tree was the tarantula.

Harry had learned some Tarantulian— well, some tarantula signals, anyway— when they'd all been in their hard-air prisons together. Now he sent an unmistakable Tarantulian signal.

"Stop right there if you know what's good for you!"

The tarantula stopped, crouching just below them. They were in the best position. They could easily have rushed down and attacked her from each side. She looked up at them with her wicked little eyes.

Suddenly George nudged Harry.

"Hey! That's *our* tarantula!"

"It can't be!"

"It is!"

They dropped onto all forty-two legs and peered down at the great spider. She peered up at them. Slowly and carefully, she sent a signal. "I'm not hunting."

They relaxed. That signal was something everyone understood. It was like "a peace pact" with us—they knew they were quite safe.

They both signaled back: "We're not hunting." She looked relieved. She was gripping on tight with her feet. Climbing trees was not her best thing.

"Come here. Help," Harry signaled.

Help? Help a centipede? Puzzled but curious, the tarantula climbed up to them. She looked suspicious, even though they had promised not to harm her.

"You see Hoo-Min nest?" asked Harry.

He had to ask several times before she

understood. At last, though, she grasped what they wanted.

"No see. But know."

"You know—where we were—caught?"

She signaled yes.

"You—show—us?"

She looked at them blankly. Even from that look, they took a clear signal: "Why should I? What are you to me but enemies and food?"

Then they knew that she had followed them up the tree to catch them and had changed her mind only because she realized she couldn't hope to win against both of them. As Belinda was forever saying, quoting from Beetle: "If you hunt two, they'll hunt you."

Harry felt himself getting mad. This great ugly greedy creature knew where his home was. She could take them there—it couldn't be far or she couldn't have gotten here. He remembered her in the hard-air, glaring around, sending threatening signals about gobbling them all up.

He rose up high on his last four segments. "You show or we attack!" he signaled fiercely.

The tarantula gave a jump of fright. George got quickly in front of Harry.

"Hx! You can't break the rule!" he crackled. Harry sank back, trying to get hold of himself. Once a creature says "I'm not hunting," he can't go back on it without first giving clear warning that now he *is* hunting. It's one of the first rules among hunters.

George was not much good at other creatures' signals. He said to Harry, "Tell her she ought to help us because we were caught together."

"That's too hard—I can't signal that!" said Harry. "Anyway, she wouldn't—she's horrible."

While they were arguing, the tarantula

seized her chance, turned, and fled down the tree as fast as she could, zigzagging among the sticking-out bits.

Seeing she had a good sporting lead, Harry signaled after her: "We're hunting!" He wasn't sure if she'd got it, but anyway now the peace was broken. The two centis shot down the tree after her.

When they reached the ground they saw her making off at speed between the roots and rotting stuff on the ground, almost dancing along. She couldn't run as fast as they could. They could catch her easily. But if she turned on them, one of them at least might be *stopped*. She was poisonous, too.

Should they follow her?

They looked at each other. She was heading the way they'd been heading! Maybe she *would* lead them home!

As one centi, they ran after her. But not too fast. Just fast enough to keep her in sight.

18. An Old Friend

It should have been easy to keep the tarantula in sight. She was so large, so stripy—so easy to spot. But somehow they lost her.

It was all the rough dead stuff on the ground—a million good hiding places. Tarantulas are very good at hiding—they have to be because their enemies can see them so easily. One minute she was there, running ahead of them. The next, she'd disappeared.

They hunted around for her, poking about under bits of bark and stones—any place a large spider might hide. But they had to give up in the end.

"Well, anyway, we're much closer to home than we were," said George.

"Only if she was running the right way," said Harry. "Be like her to run a different way, just to fool us. She's a mean, horrible creature!" he added, hoping the tarantula would get the signal somehow. (She didn't, and if she had, she wouldn't have cared. She'd run up a tree and was looking down at them, and if tarantulas could laugh, she'd have been laughing.)

There was nothing for it but to keep going in the same direction. They'd been on the move all night, and now it was nearly time for them to sleep. But first they needed to eat. They hadn't eaten for two nights!

They could smell dampness nearby. They headed toward it. It turned out to be a boggy place in the forest. It smelled very strong when they got up close to it.

"Phew!" said George. "It stinks worse than those sea-cucumber eggs!"

"Never mind," said Harry sensibly. "We don't have to swim in it." The Great Dropping Damp had dampened them beautifully, so they didn't even have to roll in it. And beside it they found two lovely fat slugs, big orange-colored ones, which were very soon in their tummies. One each.

They were just going to dig themselves a day-nest when they heard a sort of trundling sound.

"I know that noise!" said Harry.

"I know that vibration!" said George.

They watched and waited. After a short time, a figure came in sight. It was familiar—as familiar as the tarantula—but much less alarming.

It was the lady dung beetle! She walked

on her front legs and with her back feet pushed a large ball of dung, bigger than herself. She looked very funny upside down, but also very happy.

Harry ran up to her. She saw him coming, and cowered behind her ball. She knew, poor thing, that there was no escape if this monster centi was hungry and wanted to eat her. (She didn't recognize him yet.)

But Harry was quick to put her at her ease.

"I'm not hunting!" he signaled cheerily. And then, as she cautiously peeped out from behind her big dung ball, he added, "It's me! Remember?"

"Good to see you! I needn't flee you!"

she signaled in Beetle (which, if you recall, always rhymes).

He didn't understand Beetle well enough to get the rhyme, but he got the message.

"Nice dung ball!" he signaled politely, waving his feelers at it approvingly.

"Yes, indeed! It's what I need," she replied. "Bigger than most, and warm as toast." (That's the best I can do. *Of course* beetles don't know about toast, but what she actually said referred to dung and I really would rather not translate it.)

"Good you got away from the Hoo-Mins all right," Harry signaled. He did this by signaling "good" and "escape" and "you" and "Hoo-Min." She got it at once.

"Hoo-Mins bad. Made me sad. Good we fled or we'd be—" She stopped on the awful word.

George gave Harry a nudge.

"Ask her how far she's come."

Harry at once understood George's idea.

"You come far?" he signaled.

The lady dung beetle waved a feeler over her back. "Gathered my ball, that is all," she said, patting untidy bits of dung with her front legs so that the ball was nice and round.

Harry felt himself growing excited. He planned his signal carefully before making it.

"You—show—us—Hoo-Min nest?"

The lady dung beetle reared back. "Go back there? I wouldn't dare! *Forward*, me. Safe, you see." And she rose on her front legs again and started to heave the ball forward.

"Please! Wait!" Harry flung himself in her path. "Me—us—home—back there! Under—Hoo-Min nest! Lost! Please! Help!"

If centipedes could fall down and beg, Harry would have done it. The lady dung beetle stopped. She was leaning against the ball, obviously longing to start trundling it away. There was a long signal-less-ness (which we'd call a silence).

"I can't go, that I know," she signaled at last. "But ball makes track. Take you back." And she gave a mighty push and started her ball rolling forward again.

The centis didn't stop her. They watched her until she disappeared.

George was thoughtful. "I sort of hope," he said, "that that big ugly dung beetle I stopped wasn't a friend of hers." Then he forgot her.

They concentrated on the ground. Yes! There was a track! A long, faint, flattened mark in the soft earth near the bog. And now they knew that the nasty tarantula had been leading them astray. The track led off at right angles to the way she'd been going.

"Follow the dung-ball track!" they crackled together.

19. The Dung-Ball Track

The track wasn't easy to follow.

On soft earth it was quite clear. But the dung beetle had pushed the ball over dry leaves and all the natural litter (not the sort dirty Hoo-Mins drop) that lay rotting on the ground. Sometimes she'd pushed it over flat stones. But usually there were traces of dung left behind which they could smell.

(Dung, as I'm sure you realize, is quite noisome, which oddly enough doesn't mean "noisy," it means "smelly." "Nasty-smelly" at that.)

Nevertheless, sometimes they lost it. Then they had to quest to and fro, feelers feeling, till one of them found it again.

They had their heads so close to the ground, following the beetle's dung trail, that they didn't realize they were also following the bog. They came to a little rise in the ground and the bog stayed below. Suddenly Harry raised his head and tested the air with his feelers.

"Grndd! Smell that!"

"I am smelling it."

"Not the dung, the bog smell! It's gone!"

"Well, what do you expect? We've left it behind."

"No, but now it's gone, don't you notice something?"

"Oh, *what?*" said George crossly.

"You know what I think?"

"I wish you'd *tell* me!"

"That wet stuff. I think that's where the Hoo-Min's water comes out. You know, when the water-post came down the Up-Pipe and nearly washed us away—I think it comes out here, because before, I could smell Hoo-Min. I was so busy with the dung smell, I didn't notice it till it stopped!"

George was listening hard now.

"If that's true," he said, "we should be very close to the Hoo-Min nest."

With hope in their hearts, they ran on, up the slope. As they came to the top of a little sandy hill, they stopped. If centipedes could whoop with joy, they would have whooped!—because just ahead of them was the Hoo-Min nest. It jutted out of the ground and looked to them like a huge termites' nest with straight sides and a flat top with a little tree thing on it with white-choke (as they called smoke) coming out of it.

And they knew that underneath the Hoo-Min nest, down the Up-Pipe (which we would call a shower drain) was—home.

First, they did a little circle-dance around each other for sheer joy and relief. Then they twisted their feelers together, which meant: "We made it and we did it together!"

Then they raced onward and downward. They knew their home tunnels

would come into smell any minute! Soon, soon, they would be safe, they would be with Belinda, eating good food and sleeping again under their damp, comfortable leaves!

But it was not to be.

As they drew level with the Hoo-Min nest, their way was suddenly—shockingly—barred.

Something came down in front of them. A straight-up-hard-thing. They pulled up sharply. They turned. They tried to flee. But there was a straight-up-hard-thing there, too!

In front of them, behind them—and, yes!—on either side—their escape was blocked.

"Hx! What's happening?" crackled George in a panic.

"I don't know! Let's climb out!"

But when they tried, they found the top was blocked. Wherever they tried to climb the straight-up-hard-thing, they were pushed back and they fell. It was *horrible.* They hurt themselves. After a while they stopped trying to climb out. They went into a corner of the closed-in place and tried to hide.

Their journey had been made much more tiring and difficult by all the dead leaves, branches, palm fronds, and other dry litter that they'd had to climb over. But all those things would have made good hiding places if they'd needed one. Only they didn't, because nothing was trying to get them. Not then.

Now they were on open, smooth ground. There was nowhere to hide. And they knew—they just *knew*—that they were in a trap.

They tried to dig a tunnel, but before they could get started, the sandy soil under them was scooped up (by a spade, as it happened, but the centis didn't know that). Then they were turned head over back feelers. The centis found themselves covered with earth. When they dug themselves out and felt around, their hearts simply sank.

They were back in prison.

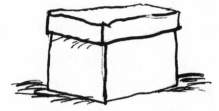

20. Wanted-for Squashing

It wasn't hard-air this time. It was worse.

There was no light—not that they minded the dark, but they couldn't see out and they couldn't signal. The sides of their prison were solid. They were in a cardboard box, but they didn't know that. They just knew they were caught. Again! Just when they'd nearly reached home!

The box prison jounced and jolted as they were carried along, under the arm of a Hoo-Min. Not that they knew they were under his arm, but they guessed a Hoo-Min had caught them because they could smell the strong, sharp, frightening smell of one. Besides, what other creature was strong, big, and cunning enough to slam the trap down on top of them, cutting off their escape in every direction?

They huddled together. This time they were *both* close to despair. Neither could comfort the other. It was awful.

The trap stopped moving as it was laid on the ground.

The centis rushed around inside it, looking for a way out. They reached upward, standing on their last four pairs of legs. They smelled, they felt, they feelered. There was no escape. None at all.

They heard those funny loud sounds—Hoo-Min voices. No way could they hope to understand Hoo-Min noise signals, but the vibrations from them were so scary that they crouched down close together.

"What are they signaling?"

Harry didn't bother to answer. How

could they possibly know what the Hoo-Mins were saying?

But you can know, because I'll tell you.

"Well, I've found what I was looking for," said the Hoo-Min that had trapped them. "A pair of them, half-grown, very fine specimens. I was lucky to catch them both at once—they don't usually run in pairs."

"Well, don't bring them indoors, that's

all. My wife will have a fit if she sees them, after her accident with the scorpion. And don't tell my son, either."

"Why, is he scared of poisonous centipedes?"

"No. Not at all. I wish he were! Then perhaps he wouldn't be so keen on collecting them. What do you want them for, anyway?"

"Oh, it's just an experiment. I've read that centipedes let off a terrible smell when you squash them, and I want to see if it's true."

"Interesting! What are you going to do, step on them?"

"No, I thought I'd hit them with a mallet. On a table or something, so I can put my face over them and get the full effect of the smell, close to."

"Not in my house, I hope!"

"No, no. I'll take them back to my place. First thing tomorrow morning."

Aren't you glad Harry and George couldn't understand that? They were frightened enough already.

The Hoo-Mins went into the house and closed the door. The box was left on the porch. On the floor.

It was the middle of the night, the

centis' most active time. They couldn't keep still. They ran around for hours inside the box, trying in vain to escape. This made a noise that could be heard for quite a long way—a rustling sound, telling the world there was something alive in that box.

And that noise attracted a hungry hairy biter.

"Hairy biter" was the centipedes' word for anything large and hairy that prowled about looking for prey. Dogs. Cats. Rats. Monkeys. And the creature that heard them rustling  and now came moseying along to investigate.

It was a big, shambling, dirty, greedy old honey badger.

Oh, I know, badgers are supposed to be

lovely animals. But let me tell you that if one of them tore or dug his way into your chicken run and gobbled up all your baby chicks, you wouldn't be very pleased. (It happened to me, so I know.)

And if you were a frightened centi, trapped in a box, you wouldn't think badgers were so lovely if you heard one slowly shuffling its way toward you with its snout snuffling and its great claw-studded front paw reaching out to see if it could break the box or knock the lid off and get to you.

21. Who Goes There?

There was a pause, which seemed like a lifetime to the two centis huddled in the box.

Then the box moved! The top of it lifted, and the big ugly snout of the hairy biter was stuck up under it. The lid fell off and the centis could feel the cool night air blow in on them.

They cowered. They could smell the creature now as well as feel its vibrations. Its great head was hanging over the top of the box. It was an enormous hairy monster! They backed in terror into the farthest corner.

"This is it, Grndd. This is the end of us," crackled Harry despairingly.

"Looks like it," said George. "Thanks for being my friend, Hx."

The hairy biter rose up on its hind legs and put its heavy front paws on the top edge

of the box. The whole box fell on its side.

They could escape now! They could run straight out of the box.

"Run, Grndd!" crackled Harry.

But neither of them moved. They were afraid to. The hairy biter was there. One move and it would grab them. It was looking at them with its little piggy eyes, as if trying to decide which of them to eat first.

What it was actually doing was thinking, *Those things taste bad. Am I hungry enough to eat them?*

But suddenly something happened that changed everything.

Badgers don't have much of a voice; normally they just grunt. But now it squealed and reared up. Something had bitten it, right where it hurt! And the creature that had bitten it had to move fast to avoid being bitten in turn, as the badger's teeth snapped right behind it.

Luckily that creature—the thing that had bitten the badger's bottom—was something that could move very fast indeed.

What runs fast? Well, who doesn't know that by now! What else but a centipede?

But why should a passing centipede risk biting a dirty great badger's hairy bottom?

Well, you see, it wasn't just any centipede.

It was a centipede who had heard rumors that two centis were trapped in a straight-side-thing, outside the Hoo-Min's nest. A special centipede who for days had been searching and hunting and asking and doing everything she could to find Harry and George. A brave mother centipede who had never given up hope.

Belinda.

And as she crept up to the box in the night to see if the trapped centis could be *her* centis, she saw the badger topple the box. She smelled her own dear son Harry and her own dear adopted son George. It was them! She'd found them at last! But almost too late!

Without a thought for her own safety, she dashed to the rescue. She swarmed up the badger's black furry tail, and pushed her way among its thick bristly hairs.

It felt her there, and turned its snout to snap at her.

Now a honey badger has very loose skin, but it's also *very* thick. Belinda had to use all her strength to pierce it. She closed her poison pincers with all her might in the fleshy part of its rear end.

Well, that certainly made up the badger's mind about whether to eat Harry and George—or indeed any other centipede—ever again. It let out another squeal and made off as fast as it could, turning every now and then to snap at the painful place where Belinda had bitten it.

And while the hairy biter ran away, Belinda rushed into the box. "Pride-of-my-basket! Best-in-my-nest!" she crackled, swarming all over Harry in transports of happiness and relief. "Oh my sweet Hxzltl! My dear little Grnddjl! Come to my feelers!"

And you can be sure they did.

But the hugging and kissing (centipede-style) didn't last long. They were all eager to get out of the trap, away from the Hoo-Min's nest. Belinda led the way, and they raced after her through the familiar smells and sounds to the nearest entrance tunnel, down it as fast as their three-times-forty-two legs would carry them, tumbling at last into their own beloved nest, where their leaves and all that meant home to them waited.

"Oh, Grndd!"

"Oh, Hx!"

"We're home! We're home! We're home!"

Every night since Harry had disappeared, Belinda had prepared food for him in case he came back, and then gone out to hunt for him. So now there was a good feast of locust, toad's legs, and a slug each for dessert.

While they ate, they told their story to Belinda, who listened, mouthparts agape in wonder and horror at their adventures.

She didn't know whether to praise them or scold them. But in the end she did neither. She just rubbed her head against theirs and stroked them with her feelers—what else could she do? She was so happy to have them home again.

But long after they'd gone to their leaves, Belinda stood guard over them and thought to herself, *I wish I could stop them from ever going out of our tunnels again! I wish I could keep them from danger!* But she knew she couldn't. Centis will be centis and there wasn't a thing she could do about it.

Who would be a mother? she thought. And then answered, "I would. . . ."

And she gave them both a centipede kiss and went contentedly to sleep.